IF ONLY SUOMI

by

ALUN BUFFRY

IF ONLY SUOMI
by
Alun Buffry
Published by ABeFree Publishing, 2020

ISBN 9781916310773

Appreciation

Thanks to Jacqui Malkin for the sketches of Suomi and to Rocky van de Benderskum for help with the cover. https://www.benderskum.rocks/
Thanks to Yorkshire Evening News website for some of the photographs from 1972.
Thanks to Lisa McKenna and Steve Land for proof reading.
Thanks to ABeFree Publishing for formatting the soft-back edition.
http://www.buffry.org.uk/abefreepublishing.html

ABOUT THE AUTHOR

Alun Buffry was born in South Wales in 1950 and lived there until 1968 when he moved to Norwich to study chemistry at the University of East Anglia. He graduated in 1971.

After leaving University, he travelled overland to India on what became known as The Hippie Trail, with little money or guidance and where he became ill.

After he returned to Norwich, he became a follower of Prem Rawat, known in those days as Guru Maharaji and he remains a follower today.

BY THE SAME AUTHOR

	ISBN
From Dot to Cleopatra: History of Ancient Egypt	9781887291098
All About My Hat: The Hippy Trail 1972	9780993210709
Time for Cannabis: The Prison Years 1991 to 1995	9780993210761
Damage and Humanity in Custody	9781533026224
Out of Joint: 20 Years of Campaigning for Cannabis	9781508420217
Myhat in Egypt: Through the Eyes of A God	9780993210778
The Effie Enigma; The Motherless Mothers	9780993210792
Inside My Hat and Other Heads	9781916310704
Words of Weed and Wisdom	9781916310766

CONTENTS

IN MEMORY OF PADDY DONNELLY

INTRODUCTION

Most books are considered to be fiction or non-fiction or a combination, written before or after the events therein. Those are either historical, which can include a lot of speculation and guesswork; simply made up, futuristic, speculative, prophecies or wishful thinking. This book is all of that. It's questionable when exactly it was written. It is clearly written after events in the author's life, but both before and after the present day. in 2020, on our calendars.

It includes memories and dreams, prophecies and wishful thinking. In fact, some sort of time travel. If only in the mind.

So what is the difference between dreams and memories?

We can have memories of dreams and dreams of memories.

We can have dreams within dreams.

What is the difference between reality and illusions or imagination? Dreams can seem very real and what we normally call reality can often seem unreal.

Ancient religions tell us that the world is nothing but an illusion, just at twinkle in the eye of the Creator, a cutting from the fingernail of Krishna, ‘Maya’.

“All the world's a stage. And all the men and women merely players.” wrote William Shakespeare.

As children we sang

“Row, row, row your boat,
Gently down the stream,
Merrily merrily, merrily, merrily,
Life is but a dream.”

Modern-day scientists may tell us that the whole Universe and everything around us, even our own bodies, is made of subatomic particles, too small to see with the naked eye, and waves, that sometimes it may be a particle and sometimes a wave, wave-particle duality and, according to the Heisenberg Uncertainty Principle, we can never say exactly when and where a particle is. They say that it is mostly space and that it is our senses and brains that put it all together so we can live in it. In other words; an illusion.

Others even say that technically it is all holographic! We are not actually here at all!

And some religious folk who believe in an all-powerful God may say that it was all made not so long ago, to look like it is much older, like a film set or a game of Dungeons and Dragons.

Then there are dreams within dreams.

Chapter 1: The Arrival 1972

Al found himself naked in a strange bed, in a strange room, alone

As he rubbed his eyes, trying to escape from the nightmare and deal with this new reality, he felt lost. He had no idea where he was or even when he was. Yet somehow he felt sort of younger.

He looked around the small room, seeking out his clothes and his phone. Nowhere to be seen. Strangely enough he saw a pair of spectacles on the bedside table. They reminded him of the heavy glass dark-rimmed ones he used to wear. He put them on. He could see through them clearly!

He spotted an open wardrobe and grabbed himself a clean pair of jeans and shirt, underwear and socks. It fitted well. He'd lost a lot of weight. Several stone in fact. Probably all that climbing he thought, but no, wait a minute, that was just a dream.

He left the room and quickly found a toilet where he emptied his now bursting bladder and then his bowels. That made him feel better and sort of brought him more back to reality. Then he looked in the mirror over a sink. He saw himself and was shocked! His hair was long and dark again as was his beard. His face was thinner and he looked, well he looked like a 22 year-old again, not the 78-year-old man he had been. Surely another dream.

Al wondered how he could wake himself up again and where he would find himself. His last memory, although vague and unreal in itself, was of 2028 in Leeds. What had he been trying to do. He had been with the wheelchair-bound Daniel, a man in his 80's and his elderly but beautiful wife, Rachel or was it Rebecca? Something about Daniel wanting to be healed. Something about a car crash. Something about a new life for the couple, before they died, Daniel had said.

Al left the bathroom, feeling very unsure and shaky about what was happening and went down the stairs towards the music and voices he could hear. It sounded like Pink Floyd.

As he entered the kitchen dining room he saw three people, two young men and a pretty young woman with long red hair. One of the men had long black hair and a long straggly beard. He other man looked a little older and remarkably like the younger version of Al's friend, Paddy, whom he had known for decades. He looked at Al and smiled and said "At last, you're awake. Want a pipe?" and passed Al a small metal pipe containing a smouldering residue or what was obviously cannabis resin. That smell was so familiar to Al, but the 'older Al', he real Al back, or rather forward, in 2028, had not toked for years. But this was just a dream so why not.
So as Paddy busied himself preparing a breakfast of bacon and eggs, toast, fruit pancakes and lots of tea

and coffee, the four of them passed along the hash pipe which Paddy filled again as soon as it was burned out. Al got high, very high, and it felt so good again, but did not ease his feeling that this was all just a dream. Although this man who said his name was Paddy, looked and sounded like the Paddy Al had known in the 1970's, of course he couldn't be. Whatever it looked like, Al knew he was in his bed dreaming in Leeds 2028. But then again, he wondered what was real and what was a dream. Maybe his whole life was a dream. Maybe he was dying and reliving it, as people said one's life flashed before one's eyes at the end.

Otherwise he had, in fact, travelled backwards in time.

That made him think he had read about time travel for the super-rich in 2028, a means of revisiting the past. But he could never have afforded that.

The other two people, Daniel and Becky, as Daniel called her, said little but laughed a lot, saying how they remembered this or that track from the several music albums Paddy was playing on an old vinyl LP record player.

As well as Pink Floyd, there was Fleetwood Mac, Caravan, Jimi Hendrix, Joni Mitchel and Bob Dylan. It was just SO good being stoned with these people, enjoying these classic sounds and even singing along to some.

Foxey Lady was one of Al's all-time favourites; memories started to flood back into Al's still foggy brain;

it reminded him of an old girlfriend from the time he had travelled to India in 1972, by the name of Diane; and Joni Mitchell reminding him of his Canadian girl friend, he had met in Afghanistan and travelled from Lahore to Delhi with, Miriam. He had not seen either girl since 1972 but had often wondered what had happened to them.

They'd be grannies now, probably, if they were still alive. He half expected one of them to walk into this dream room.

Al remembered now that he had written the story of his overland trip to India and back in his book, self-published in 2014, called 'All About My Hat, the Hippy Trail, 1972'. It had been fun writing but it had never been a best seller. It was supposed to have been written by the hat that Al had been given by a barber in Greece and Al had worn it to India and back to the UK to Norwich. Al wondered where that hat was now. He also wondered if he had written it, would write it, or whether that was just another dream within a dream? How could he be here and on his way to India at the same time?

Al decided to ask dream Paddy what was going on. It was seeming strange that he was dreaming, if he was dreaming, yet knowing it was a dream and it had all started to become very real. What was the dream? Going to India or being here. Had he been to India and come back and then come here? Or had he never actually been to India at all. Did he live here or in Norwich? And if this was Leeds, was it 1972 or 2028.

Was it some sort of joke or scam? Who was this Paddy? The Paddy he knew, or thought he knew, died in 2014 or so, aged about 75. Was he, Al, really just 22, or a 78-year-old man dreaming? Would he wake up? How could he make himself wake up? This was all doing his head in, especially after the pipes of hash. Maybe he was in some sort of mental asylum.

“Paddy, I am really confused! I am not sure what I am doing here. I’m not even sure that I am here at all!

“Are you the same Paddy I met in Norwich in 1974? What’s going on?

Paddy chuckled: “That I don’t know, I’m no prophet, man! I don’t know the future, only what you visitors tell me and that ain’t much.

“Anyway it’s only 1972 so I don’t even know about next year. I never met you before Al, but I do live in Norwich sometimes. Is that where you’re from, ‘cos that’s where Daniel and Becky are going? They can’t stay here. They can’t risk meeting their other selves or anyone that knows them, that could be a disaster, who know what could happen, man. But if you lived in Norwich, well you can’t go there. Have you ever lived here, in Leeds?”

“No,” said Al, “Never been in Leeds, except one for an afternoon in about 2004. You trying to tell me it’s 1972 again? I went to India in 1972, left Norwich in February for about nine months. How can I be here if I’m heading for India? What’s the date anyway, what day is it supposed to be?"

"Yep, 1972, Leeds it is, to be sure, Friday 26th of May.

"Leeds just beat Arsenal one nil in the FA Cup Final a few weeks ago. That was a good match. I went to Wembley to see it.

"Your other self is probably off to India about now, what date did you leave?

"But you can't go there now anyway, people would think it strange if you've left then turn up again and if you haven't left there'll be two of you to be sure!"

Al was even more confused.

"If it's end of the May 1972, I should be in Afghanistan or somewhere, with Keith, smoking chillums! So I wouldn't be in Norwich anyway, or Leeds."

Al started to remember more. He had been an old man, seventy-eight years of age, living in Norwich where he had met an older Daniel and Rebecca. He had gone to Leeds with them and been somehow sent back in time to 1972. He started to remember his long life bother before and after 1972, some of the many places that he had visited and people that he had met. It was like his life was flashing before his eyes, like he was dying.

"You'd better spend your seventy-two hours here then man.," continued Paddy.

“I’ll give you some money and you can explore the city. There’s a music festival on in the Roundhay park about two miles out, you can walk it or get a bus from near the station. Daniel and Becky were going to drive to Norwich with you but you can’t go now.

“Maybe they’d better not go there either, they might meet people who know the other you!”

Al stood up and said, rather loudly: “So I’m back in time, I can change the future! Just can’t remember much about between now and 2028 which I think it was yesterday. How do I know what to change? I can’t remember what date we left Norwich in the van, there were five of us.” said Al rather enthusiastically.

“I don’t know nothing about Leeds? Can I phone my parents?”

“No you can’t change anything, man, too many complications. Better not phone anyone.

“You’ll like it here, Leeds ain’t bad. Roundhay Park is massive and there’ll be a band playing. It’s got lakes and woods and a couple of little cafés, even an outdoor swimming pool. It’s over five hundred acres to wander. And you can nip into Woolies, you know Woolworth's, there’s a nice little café and a record lounge place. And there’s Seacroft Market, I often go there, buy some grub when I’m in Leeds. And the river Aire is good in places too.

“I’ll give you a street map. You can check out the music

bar in Woolies. It's on High Street, just up the road, easy to find.

"And Donovan's on at the University tomorrow."

"I'm going to give you fifty quid spending money, should last you. You can crash here for the nights if you want. Just make sure you're back before midnight on Sunday or you may turn into a pumpkin.

"Seriously though, if you miss the deadline you might not get back at all."

Paddy continued.: "You know Jackie Charlton plays for Leeds United. He was in the sixty-six world cup team. Maybe he's in town and you can get his autograph, post it anonymously to yourself, ha! You're other self wouldn't know who sent it.

"But Daniel said he wanted to change things so he would avoid a nasty car crash that cripples him in the 1980's but he can't do that, I told him already. They're driving to Norwich in my red Triumph Herald. I'll pick it up next week when I get back. I'll go on the train.

"See, man, there's two of him now, the one living in Leeds that will crash and the one in the house now and going to Norwich. And two Becky's too. It may be that our Daniel may avoid a crash and avoid being crippled. They'll be living new lives for sure but we don't know what's going to happen. He mustn't try to stop the other Daniel's crash; that could mean he never had any reason to come back and won't be here to stop it. We just don't know enough about that type of paradox. If he had stopped it, you wouldn't be here either. Fuck it's complicated.

"Maybe he'll crash anyway, maybe he'll never get to Norwich. Maybe he'll stay with Becky, maybe he won't. None of us know our futures. I don't know yours any more than you do. I just know that they came for a new life and you came for seventy-two hours. God, if I knew more I'd be a millionaire.

"You people that I host never tell me nothing much. It's up to you what you do. If you're going back to wherever you come from, you got to be back here by midnight February, it's the 26h now and you've been here eleven hours already. Just enjoy it and don't make any contact with anyone you know!"

Of course, Al from 2028 knew far more about Paddy than Paddy knew about himself. He knew, for instance, that Paddy had sadly passed away over a decade earlier, after suffering from Prostate Cancer for several years. He'd better now tell Paddy that, he thought.

In 2010 they had been to, or would go to, Luxor together with another friend, for two weeks. They stayed in a small bungalow. By then they had been good friends for decades in the grounds of a hotel on Kings Island. When they had arrived, in February, the temperature was a lovely 23 degrees. A week later it was 38, too hot to move, but before then had managed to visit the Temples of Luxor and Karnak, which was one of if not the largest temples in the world, built by various pharaohs over a thousand years. They went to the Sound and Light show.

They also visited the Souk, and had crossed the Nile to the West Bank to see the great mortuary temple of Hatshepsut, the Ramasseum and several tombs in the Valley of the Kings.

At the hotel they both ate copiously in the serve-yourself buffet three times a day.

Paddy had taken with him a small piece of Moroccan hash so each evening they had a smoke, using an upturned glass over smouldering hash on a pin.

Al remembered that when he had first met Paddy, in 1974. Al was looking for somewhere else to live and Paddy arrived at a mutual friend's house, saying he had a house for rent. Without further ado, Paddy became Al's landlord for a five-bedroomed house for six months or so. There are many tales to tell of what went on in that house, but that's for some other time. Paddy had been running one of the two 24-hour cafes in Norwich but had closed it. It had been on Kings Street. An apt name. For most of the time that Al knew Paddy, he lived on a converted coach and travelled between Morocco, Spain, France, England and the Ireland. Eventually, in the early twenty-first century, he was "set up" and arrested in Morocco at the point of exporting a large amount of cannabis on his bus. He spent a couple of years there in prison in Tangiers, also suffering from prostate cancer. Paddy had five children, with three mothers. he looked after them all.

Chapter 2: Day One

So Al decided to go out and stroll round the area and find his bearings, something he usually did when he arrived in a new place. They had actually been in a flat above a small ironmongers shop on a busy main road.

So Al just strolled down the street and when he saw a bus stop, took a bus to the city centre. The fare was remarkably little. It took about an hour, but was quite boring. The bus stopped at the main railway station and Al got off.

The streets were noisy and crowded with both people and traffic. Just a big busy city. Leeds, he knew, had been and maybe still was one of the biggest cities in England after London and maybe Birmingham. It had been an important city at least since the times of the Industrial Revolution with its products carried along the lengthy Leeds and Liverpool canal. It was hardly used for that purpose any more, but he thought it may be possible to take a boat along it, or else walk some way. He could see on the map that the canal went close to the station.

In earlier times, Leeds was important for wool and flax and then had lots of cotton mills and other factories.

It was quite a warm and dry day, warm, so strolling

round was an option. He bought a copy of the local paper but soon lost it, as he strolled around the crowded train station where he went to see some old steam engines.

There were still some pulling passenger and goods trains back then as well as diesels. But it was too crowded and he soon left back out on to the street.

He could see by the map that the City square was one side of the station and the River Aire was on the other, so he went to the Square first, thinking it would be quaint.

Then he went back and left on the other side of the station and walked down Princess Street towards the river. It was not far.

The people he saw seemed all in a rush, many carrying large bags of shopping and most looked unfriendly and miserable. He was not enjoying this city at all. He wondered why on Earth of all places he had chosen to come to Leeds. But then maybe he hadn't been given a choice as that is where Daniel and Rebecca were coming to and they were paying for him. But since arriving here they had kept themselves to themselves and left him to do his own thing. Paddy was friendly, jolly and hospitable but that did not include acting as a guide or showing him the city. Maybe Paddy didn't like Leeds much either.

It would be good if I could find some company, he thought, but I'll have to be careful. I''m supposed to know about the last 20 years or so but not the next 56! I mustn't even hint at future events, not that I can remember much detail. Stay away from politics. Don't mention Thatcher or Bush or Bin Laden, or the Twin Towers and the wars. In 1972 they're still worried about World Wars and Vietnam, let alone Iraq, Afghanistan, Syria and Korea. Half the world was starving and the Cold War was far from over. It's only nine years since Kennedy was killed and they don't yet know who did it. And of course time travel was limited to fiction. I am going to say as little as I can.

After a very brief look at the river, he went back to the station again for a cup of tea in the station canteen.

Then he visited a small outdoor market not far from the station. Cheap items that would be almost antiques in 2028, if he could take them back. Collectables like Dinky Cars, old tins, silver jewellery, so much more.

He saw a sign at a petrol station that read 35P a Gallon.

He decided to head for Hyde Park. Paddy had said that was an area popular with students. It was an area between the University and a district called Headingley.

He passed the City Square and saw the Town Hall and the entrance to the City Museum but he did not go in.

But when he got there it wasn't a park at all.

It was streets of Victorian back-to-back terraced housing, almost a slum.

He decided to check out the prices in a local food store. Bread, ten pence a loaf. English money was already decimalised. The coins were halfpenny, one pence, two pence, five and tens and a fifty pence coin. Notes were £1, £5 and £10. Probably larger denominations but not so common.

Milk was five pence; a jar of coffee for thirty pence; a box of Cornflakes for eleven pence; a dozen eggs for twenty; two pounds of sugar ten pence; crisps were three pence a bag. He bought a bag. It had the old little blue bag of salt in.

But then again, he thought, I had only earned twenty pounds a week for five days and Saturday morning.

His grant at UEA had been ten pounds a week and his rent three of four. And that was just for thirty weeks each year; he had to be looked after by his parents or find a summer job. Out of that he had to buy his food and drink, clothes, transport, books and entertainment. But he had gotten through it. He went back to the train station to drink some more tea.

As he sat there sipping, he thought he heard two women talking. One was saying “Elaine Silver it was, said some guy from the future was here. If we can find him we can get the soccer results and get rich. Bet he knows a thing or two that’ll come in handy.”

With that he left to get a green bus away from the crowds. Were they talking about him or Daniel or were there others here.

After all, others must have come back even from beyond 2028; if everyone was supposed to keep the secrets who would know? But then again, there's always one to break the fucking rules.

And who made the rules anyway and did anyone police them? Were there Time Police? Were they watching him.

As he sat on the bus he spotted a discarded local Leeds newspaper. That gave him an idea. He could sort of change the future past without really changing anything.

When he got off the bus he found a post office on the High Street.

He tore off some newspaper which included the top of the front page with the date and name of the paper. He got an air mail envelope from the counter and put a ten pound note inside the newspaper and into the envelope.

He sealed the envelope and wrote on the front his own name and Poste Restante, New Delhi, India. That was one way to send mail to somebody abroad, so they could pick it up at the main post office in the city it was sent to. He asked the price of a first class stamp and was told it cost three pence. In 2028 it was almost three pounds!

It wasn't even changing anything at all because, he remembered, he did receive a ten pound note from Leeds in New Delhi and it had helped him tremendously when he had no money at all.

BANK of ENGLAND
HU41 643192
I Promise to pay the Bearer on Demand the sum of
1
One Pound
Elizabeth R
1
LONDON
For The Gov. and Comp. of the BANK of ENGLAND
Chief Cashier
HU41 643192

BANK OF ENGLAND
I Promise to pay the Bearer on Demand the Sum of
66E 295660
5
Five Pounds
5
London
For the Gov. and Comp. of the Bank of England
Chief Cashier
66E 295660

BANK OF ENGLAND
I Promise to pay the Bearer on Demand the Sum of
A10 883037
10
TEN Pounds
London
for the Gov. and Comp. of the BANK OF ENGLAND
10
CHIEF CASHIER
A10 883037

That was still a month or so away in 1972 time but in his memories it had already happened.

That was one of the two ten pound notes he collected, or had collected, or would collect, or whatever, that day. One had been from a friend in Norwich and the other, well he had always wondered who he knew in Leeds that had sent it.

That was a 56 year old mystery solved.

He briefly thought of buying some stuff now and burying it so he could dig it up again in 2028, if he ever actually got back.

He wouldn't tell Paddy though.

Then Al went back to Paddy's flat. Paddy cooked a good meal of fish, pasta and vegetables with a bottle of good red wine.

Then they went in Paddy's car to a pub called The Fforde Grene on Roundhay Road. It was a drive of about half an hour.

The pub, a large and old building, had a rock band playing and it was crowded.
It was very smoky. This was well before the smoking ban in public places. People were smoking joints as well as cigarettes.

Paddy knew one of the barmen who also brought the beers up from the cellar, name of Jimmy and Al drank a couple of pints of his old favourite, Newcastle brown beer. Al saw that Guinness and Newcastle Brown were twenty pence a pint each and most of the other beers like Double Diamond, which he also used to drink, were eighteen.

Paddy filled and lit a hash pipe, he took a puff and passed it to Al. He also took a puff. It felt so good. It was good hash in these days.

There was a jukebox and when the band finished playing Paddy put some coins in. The song 'Metal Guru' by T. Rex which was apparently number 1 in the charts. Al remembered his 'other self' or was it just him, had seen them at UEA in Norwich a couple of years earlier when they were still called Tyrannosaurus Rex.

He had seen lots of good bands in those days at UEA.

That was one of the best few hours that Al had in Leeds until then. They went back to "Paddy's Pad", as he called it and smoked several hash pipes.

"How does it work, Paddy?" asked Al, "Bringing us back here through time like this?"

"I don't really know," he replied, "it's something to do with genetic code, so I was told, something about sending the essential person back though a time tunnel and reassembling them here with a machine called a 4D printer that they sent back the instructions for. Then they build a new body and bring you here in the night. It's beyond me, I am not a scientist. I was told that at the start they just buried messages so somebody in the future could work it all out. Then, when it's time for you to go back, you take a sleeping potion and they come and pick you up and send you back. I don't get to see any of that. They said they can't send me to the future because the future me would have to come back here first and they won't tell me anything about the future. I might be dead by 2028."

Al went to sleep, his mind still reeling, still wondering at the miracle of time travel.

Chapter 3: Day Two 1972

The next morning, Saturday May 27, Al awoke early enough, about eight o'clock. He had been dreaming again, a very surreal dream where he was in India with his friend Suomi. He thought it weird. They were both young again. He wondered briefly what was real and what was a dream. Now it felt dreamy but real. He pinched himself. Yes, he felt that, so he got out of bed. He was alone.

He suddenly remembered he was really in 2028. Then he remembered he was in 1972, in Leeds and had come backwards through time and was young again. Then he remembered that Paddy had said there were now two of him, this one and the other 'original' Al who was on his way to India. That didn't make sense. Paddy had said this Al had to go back to 2028 and that was tomorrow, Sunday.

Al figured that if he left the bedroom and found Paddy, he'd know what was real and what was a dream. Yet a few times before, he remembered, this Al had awoken from a dream only to find that he was still dreaming, and it was said that life itself was just a dream, just an illusion, some sort of trip. Maybe that was it.

That was it, he was in some sort of dream trip, layer on

layer and that made him feel lost, out of control, living a dream life at the whim of some sort of supernatural comic controller. He felt weird. He'd never felt like this is all his 78 years, with or without drugs.

He washed in a basin on the table in the room using the water from a large jug and dressed quickly then went to the kitchen where Paddy was sat reading the paper besides a massive pot of tea on the table.

Paddy made eggs and toast and beans and they drank tea and chatted. Daniel and Becky appeared about nine o'clock and chatted a while and then set off in the Triumph. They had decided to go to India, overland instead of Norwich, where they could just disappear. First they would go to London and get some money together then they would catch the 'Magic Bus' Al didn't want to tell him that his other self was in fact on his way to India; partly because he was not sure that he was, or whether he was just here in Leeds, or in Leeds and in Afghanistan at the same time, or if there were now two of him!. He thought again of his friend John Sullivan. Was John dead or was he still alive? The Al in Afghanistan would not yet have known, yet the AL from 2028 now in 1972, did!

Paddy told Al that America had just launched a spaceship to Venus, called the Varana 8.

Al also learned that Edward Heath was the Tory Prime Minister, not that he cared. That was, after all, just history and he could do nothing about it, even if he wanted to.

They smoked a couple of hash pipes and Al was stoned again.

Al mused that here in 1972, there were no household computers and few colour TV's. No internet and no mobile phones, Ipods or Ipads. Even the list of chemical elements was shorter and there had been few space probes although men had supposedly walked on the Moon.

They still had Apartheid and the Berlin Wall in 1972.

He pondered, was the world a better place now or in 2028. What had changed? Well, he thought, in 2028 there were a heck of a lot more people for starters.

There was more money than ever, more super-rich and more desperately poor.

There was more food but more starving people in 2028.

There were more police but more crime and more prisons.

There were more schools, universities and teachers in 2028 and even on-line courses, but there were more illiterate people than ever before.

There were more doctors and hospitals but more sick people and more illnesses and even though people lived longer so many will become ill or disabled.

There was more automation but less jobs.

There was more entertainment even indoors, but more suicides.

There were more marriages either in Churches or civil, but more broken families and single parents.

There was still famine, pestilence, plagues and wars.

There was probably more integration of races and cultures but just as much bigotry and racism.

There were more commodities and consumables but more waste and pollution.

By 2028, well long before, industrialists had realised the profitability of recycling and supposedly cleaning up the rivers and oceans. They were putting so many chemicals in the tap water that water filters were essential in homes and eating places and bottled water was a major industry yet the poorest people suffered most.

Organic food was common here in 1972 but in 2028 it had its own sections in the massive supermarkets that had replaced so many of the local shops and it all cost more.

Al wondered what really changed in people? Nothing. In what ways were we better off in 2028 and in what ways were we worse off? Sure people could travel faster, if they had the money, but everyone seemed to have less time and were rushing round like mad men.

It was almost ten o'clock so Al was already thinking about lunch. He'd head for Woolworth's café. He left the building.

Then he realised of course that he didn't know whether to walk to his left or his right.

He hadn't noticed Woolies the day before so he chose left and walked up the street, marvelling at the people, the cars, buses and contents of shop windows, until he reached the end and saw the sign 'High Street'.

So, as he hadn't seen Woolies, he crossed the road and walked back up High Street on the other side. He spotted the Ironmongers shop and not long afterwards saw Woolies

There had been Woolworth's stores in many towns including his home town in Wales and Norwich and it was incredibly familiar, although they had closed all their shops late in the twentieth century – or they would, he mused. He saw, by the entrance door, a. list of the various departments including the Kwik Cafe and the Music Hall.

First some tea and food. He headed straight for the café which was quite crowded, bought himself a pot of tea with the ancient pound note that Paddy had given him, some cheese on toast and a chocolate cake.

Most of the tables were full but he spotted a table for two with one empty chair. Sat in the other chair was a pretty young girl with long blond hair. He strode over and asked her if he could sit on the empty chair.

"Oui, oui, "she said, "please sit down," in a delightful French accent.

"Merci", said Al, smiling, "You sound French. Where you from?"

"Paris," said the girl. "But now I am in Leeds at the University."

"What you studying?", asked Al.

"Chemical Engineering", she said.

"Oh I did Chemistry at UEA in Norwich, at the University of East Anglia, finished last year, BSC. Leeds was on the list of places I applied for in 1968 but I chose Norwich instead, because it is a smaller city and I liked the course better. No jobs yet though. I've lost interest a bit in Chemistry. I'm going to go travelling with some friends in a van to Turkey!"

Already Al had made a mistake, confusing himself with the Al travelling to India. At that time, *that* Al had already set off with his friends, to Turkey, with no intention of going to India, but had gone on from Turkey with his mate Keith, towards India. He sadly remembered again that his other friend, John Sullivan, had died in a crash in Turkey the night after he and Keith had left them. He hadn't even known about that until he was on his way home and ill in Afghanistan with no money. If only he could stop that happening! But what would be the consequences, Paddy had warned him about making changes.

That other Al hadn't even reached India yet but John was already dead. He didn't know what to do or say.

But maybe this slip-up telling this girl wouldn't matter. She probably never met the other Al.

He felt very comfortable with her though. Like he'd known her for ages, She was warm and he was attracted to her. His mind may be 78 years old but his body was now just 22 and she was about that age, blond, French and very sexy.

"I'm Al, what's your name?"

"Suomi" she said, "with an I on the end," and offered him her hand.

But instead of shaking it, without thinking, he took her hand, leaning forwards and kissed it.

Suomi laughed and said "Enchanté!"

"If only, Suomi," said Al.

Suomi giggled delightfully. They sat and chatted for ages, about student life, about what she liked and about stuff like the Moon landing. Al mentioned that he had been to see a lot of bands at Uni and also been to two Isle of Wight pop festivals

Suomi said that in the previous years she had seen a lot of bands at Leeds Refectory, including many of Al's own favourites: Jimi Hendrix whom Al had seen at the Isle of Wight, Pink Floyd whom Al said he had seen at Swansea University, The Who, Iron Maiden, Rod Stewart and one of Al's most favoured bands, the Moody Blues.

Clearly they had the same tastes in music but that was no surprise, many students at that time also loved those bands.

Suomi said that she had tickets to see Donovan at the University that evening, and she wanted to go to the Woolworth's Music Bar to listen to his album and maybe buy it.

"I loved the Universal Soldier album," she said. "I want to listen to Catch The Wind and maybe I buy it.

"You want to come to the Music Bar and listen to it with me?"

Al's heart skipped a beat.

"Yes please," he said.

In his mind he may be old enough be be her grandfather, In his body he was young enough for her. His heart skipped another beat as Suomi stood up in her long coloured flowery dress well below her knees. His only thought was "Wow!" She was gorgeous!

“What about your boyfriend?” asked Al.

“I don’t ‘ave one,” she replied, “We are broken. You ‘ave a girlfriend Al?

“No, not now,” Al answered, “We are broken too.”

“That is good,” she said and smiled.

They set off to find the Music Hall.

Suomi quickly found the Donovan album she wanted and they both went into one of the listening booths and put on a couple of pairs of giant headphone. Al felt good being so close to her; he sensed her breathing faster and that made him breathe faster too, as they listened to the slow acoustic guitar and voice of Donovan. He didn’t want it to end.

Suomi bought the record. Al bought an album by Jimi Hendrix, which he thought he’d give to her later. It was ‘Are You Experienced’ and had the Foxey Lady track. He hoped she did not already have it, guessing she would have said ‘I ‘ave that one’ if she had.

Then they headed back out of Woolies into the street and Suomi said “You want to come with me to the Park, the Roundhay, we can walk in the woods and maybe there is a band and maybe later we can go to see Donovan as I ‘ave two tickets and my friend she cannot come because she ‘as an illness today?”

Al just smiled and said “OK, far out”.

"We can go on bus to station and then on other bus to Park, It is about an 'our and an 'arf. It is too far for me to want to walk now. OK?

"The Roundhay Park, it is an 'undred years old now and very nice. On Monday there will be cricket match for ladies."

"Sure," said Al, let's do that!"

So they took a green double-decker bus to the train station and took another to Roundhay Park. The journey was not at all boring as the day before, as Suomi chatted away and they laughed together. The people on the bus seemed much happier and the streets less busy, even though it was now Saturday. The two bus rides went quickly and soon enough they were walking into the massive park.

Roundhay Park was indeed spacious. They spent several hours there and Al lost all track of time. On a lovely sunny day, he basked in both the sun and the shine emanating from Suomi.

They spent an hour or so slowly walking around the large lake, that Suomi said was called Waterloo and was about a "mile and un 'arf and walk and sometimes people go go on a boat ride."

There were plenty of ducks there. They sat and watched a couple of men fishing but they caught nothing.

They walked amongst the trees. They saw a rose garden and walked hand-in-hand sometimes. They briefly visited the ruins of a small castle

Then they sat and listened to a small group of young long-haired guys and a girl playing acoustic guitars and tom-tom and singing: one of their songs was Sunshine Superman, one of the few songs of Donovan that Al could actually remember. Suomi took Al's hand for that song, so he liked it even more.

At about four o'clock, as neither Al nor Suomi wore a watch, they decided to walk back into the city and take a meal in an Indian restaurant, although Suomi said she didn't like her food too spicy.

It was early evening and the restaurant was quite busy with most of the diners looking like students. Al bought a bottle of red wine. The waiter said they had three types of wine, "Red, White and Rosey" He wondered out loud if the "Rosey" was made from roses from the park, which sent Suomi into a delightful fit of giggles.

Al was enjoying himself more than he had for a long time but already regretting the *fact* that he not only had to leave in a little over a day but he also had to tell Suomi and he had to make up a reason why. He could not tell her the truth that he was from a different time and, in his mind at least, 78-years-old.

He knew he couldn't stay and he knew he couldn't take her back with him which, he realised, would rob her of her life experiences from 1972 to 2028 and he didn't want to do that. In any case, if he did, she'd probably arrive in 2028 as a 21-year old bombshell and he'd be 78, well old enough to be her grandfather. Once again he felt it all to be unreal, a dream, and expected to wake up at any time. But, he thought, I must just enjoy the present, for, as he had heard so many time, 'The Present is a Gift' and right now, it surely was.

After the meal, during which Al had eaten a hot Madras vegetable curry and Suomi a Kurma, with rice and chapati and Indian Kulfi ice creams, Al discovered that she was vegetarian, like he was, even though he sometimes ate fish. But he didn't tell her that he ate fish. The meal with wine cost just over three pounds.

It was time to head for the University refectory for the Donovan show. Al said he'd pay for the meal and she could pay for the tickets, which she had bought already anyway.

The refectory building was quite large with a dining room of it's own as well as a bar and the concert hall.

It was actually quite crowded and noisy. Al had forgotten how much noise a large group of students could make. They had to shout at each other to be heard, but that brought them closer together, almost face touching face, breathing the same air and sharing each other's aromas. Suomi smelt so good. He hoped he did too, it had ben a long day. At least she didn't back away.

When it was time for Donovan to play, it went quiet.

Everyone was seated on the floor, close together, and Al found himself close to Suomi. He put his arm round her. She did not resist.

Donovan was dressed like a hippy, with a blue shirt and silky purple pants, and sat on a cushion on the stage. He looked so young"

Although Donovan had never been one of Al's favourite singers, he had liked his stuff and he enjoyed it far more than he thought he would.

The "set" included guitar and harmonica songs by Donovan:'Catch the Wind", "The Lovely Day", "Hurdy Gurdy Man", "There is a Mountain" and one of Al's favourites, "Sunshine Superman" during which Suomi took his hand and held it tightly. All so apt, so conducive to Al's mood. Very turtle-dove.

After the concert they went to the student bar for a quick drink. The radio was playing The Mamas and the Papas song 'Dream A Little Dream Of Me'. Again so apt.

Al decided to tell Suomi that he would be leaving the following day. Inside he was crying.

"Suomi, I have only tonight here and tomorrow I have to go away and I don't want to, and I can't say where I'm going and I might not be coming back. I don't want to go. I want to stay here with you but it's impossible. I've been enjoying being with you so much but I don't know if it's best to just say goodbye now."

"Que sera, sera," she said, "that's what we say, what will be will be. I'm glad we met but nothing lasts for ever.

"Let's just make best the time what we 'ave together. I want you to come back with me to my apartment that I 'ave and spend a few 'ours together, OK?"

"I'd like to do that too," said Al, smiling. "Let's get a taxi, can we phone one?"

"Yes there's a phone box outside, it usually takes about 'alf an 'our."

So they phones for a taxi and while they waited they sat on some grass and ignored everyone and got close

together and then cuddled and Suomi kissed him.
"You 'ave a good kiss," she said.

"So have you Suomi my love".

Their kisses were soft and slow, with no sense or urgency, more sensual than sexual, but warm and more than just friendly.

They hugged and kissed again in the taxi which soon took them to High Street, not far from Paddy's flat, and went though a door and upstairs to Suomi's place, above a shop.

It was a small but cosy bedsitter. A small kitchen unit and sink at one end and a single bed at the other. There were posters on the wall, reading "Make Love Not War" and "Live for the Moment" and a poster picture of Jimi Hendrix biting his guitar strings. There was a collection of beer mats around the room and a hap-hazard notice board with gig tickets and notes.

Suomi put the kettle on the stove for coffee, then selected a vinyl LP and put it on her record player switched it on. She had chosen the Mamas and the Papa's. It played songs like 'California Dreaming' and 'Dream a Little Dream Of Me".

Whilst Suomi was making coffee, Al looked briefly through her record collection. It reminded him of his own from those days. There were albums by Pink Floyd, Caravan, Soft Machine, Peter Green, Fleetwood Mac, The Cream, Fairport Convention, Joni Mitchell,

Bob Dylan, Leonard Cohen, The Byrds, Buffalo Springfield and Hendrix. Thankfully not 'Are You Experienced' which he had carried all day and finally given to her.

He noticed a copy of the I Ching and on the table was Autobiography of a Yogi and a book about travelling to India, in French

Suomi asked Al if he wanted to smoke some hash.

"I will make a joint," she said.

Al told her he would like to smoke but not a joint as he didn't smoke tobacco.

"I haven't smoked tobacco for thirty years", he said.

Suddenly he realised he'd slipped up.

"But you are only twenty-two," laughed Suomi

"I mean thirty days", he said, "It just seems like thirty years!"
Suomi went to a shelf and picked up a jar and brought it to the small settee where Al was sitting.

"I 'ave also some grass", she said.

"You want we smoke this?"

"Yes OK."

“You roll a joint then?” She passed Al the jar and some ‘skins’ small size and Al stuck some together.

He showed Suomi how to get the seeds out easily, by crumbling it onto a record cover so they rolled off it on to the table and then he rolled it up, passed it to Suomi and offered her a light from a match.

They smoked the weed, it was strong, and almost as soon as they’d finished, she leaned towards him and started to unbutton his shirt.

“Are you sure Suomi? You know I have to leave tomorrow. I can’t stay even though I want to, And I can’t come back. We may never see each other again.”

“Yes Al, let us be making the love tonight. I ‘ave the pill, I won’t ‘ave a baby.”

So Al leaned in and they kissed. He let her remove his shirt from him then he gently unbuttoned her blouse. As it fell apart and he saw her breasts, he gasped. It had after all been decades since he’s seen such breasts close up, let alone being able to touch them.
As he and Suomi slipped onto the floor, they kissed and caressed each other and then they were both naked.

After they had made love twice that night, Al started to feel bad again, sad again.

He knew that clocks were ticking, time was passing and in less than twenty-four hours she would be gone, out of his life for ever

He wanted to laugh with joy and cry in desperation at the same time. Yet he vowed that for the rest of this night and maybe in the morning he would make their hours together as happy as he could.

He would talk with Paddy and see his options. If he had to go, so be it, but he would make Paddy swear secrecy but also promise to always look after Suomi.

He wondered if Suomi got old, could they meet again in 2028 or afterwards.

But he knew she, hopefully, had her own life to live and 56 years is a long time. Just look at what happened to me in 56 years, he thought.

He fell asleep thinking that.

The following morning was a Sunday, Al's last day.

It was 10 o'clock before they woke up in each others arms. As he drifted in and out of sleep, Suomi had gotten out of the bed they had moved to and made coffee.

"Good morning my lover," she said.

She was standing in front of him, stark naked, holding two cups of coffee.

The coffee was cold by the time they had finished sex again and Al realised it was gone noon. He had to go to see Paddy.

So he got dressed and arranged to meet her at 5 o'clock in a local café that Suomi told him about.

He would tell Paddy about Suomi, well not all about her, but about his feelings.

He would talk to Paddy and introduce him to Suomi.

Al was considering three options.

He could stay here and let his 2028 body deteriorate and die and hope to live a new life with Suomi. Of course he did not know if the relationship would last. None of Al's relationships that had started off with good intent love making had lasted very long, although he kept friends with many of the girls..

He could see if there was any chance of taking her back with him. But would she age of would she stay young and he would be old again? And would that be robbing her of her life?

Or he could do as was intended and go back alone, leaving her here to her life choices and experiences and just regard it all as a pleasant memory or dream.
He said a quick cheerio, see you later so as not to burst into tears and headed back to Paddy's place.

Paddy was sitting at his kitchen table drinking tea and smoking his hash pipe.

"Back then I see, to be sure. Did you have a good time? You look sad, what's happened?"

Al started to cry as he explained what had happened and his conundrum, his choices, his confusion, his feelings of love and despair, to Paddy. He told him how he had met Suomi and spent the time with her, that they had made love and that he had fallen into it.

He told him that he wanted to stay but knew that he shouldn't. He said that he wanted both the live a life with her but also to go back and finish his real life in the future.

He said that some things that the world went through, that he did not want to talk about, he did not want to go through again.

But he said through the good and the bad he had a life full of joy and that he had been, or would be, happy and contented in 2028, but now he wasn't so sure it would be the same for him.

And what about Suomi?

He had told her, he said to Paddy, that he was going to have to leave and probably never return and she had accepted that – but that was after a day of drinking and a smoke and a good day too.

"Have I ruined her life? Have I changed her future? Will I never know what happens to her? Paddy will you promise to always look out for her and make sure she doesn't come to any harm, if you can?

"Will you promise me that but never to tell her the truth.

And make sure she never meets the other me."

"Yes", said Paddy, "I will promise you that. But I'd say you better be going back because you know you only came for three days and people in 2028 will surely be waiting for you. You must have friends and loved ones there too, and you still have that life to live."

And now the hardest part of the story to tell.

Paddy gave Al the sleeping draught that, he said, would facilitate transfer. Al lay on top of a single bed, started to feel drowsy and drift off. He started to wonder was was happening and what had happen and what would happen and what was the difference between now and then.

He couldn't stop thinking about Suomi and he couldn't hold back the tears.

"Don't worry old man, it *will* be OK," said Paddy who was sitting besides him.

Al was thinking that the older one gets, the more one loses. He had actually been happy and fulfilled in 2028, yet now he was devastated by the thought of going back.

He remembered in the Highlander film, and in Doctor Who too, they had both said something like "The trouble with being immortal is that you lose everyone you ever loved and everyone you ever knew."

But of course Al knew that he wasn't immortal, in these worlds anyway, and would soon be dying himself and that was inevitable and should not be regretted because living for ever, well for ever was along time and one day the Sun itself would explode.

But that just made him want to cry more.

He thought again about his mother and father, grandparents, uncles and aunts, and John Sullivan who, by now in 1972, was probably already dead in Turkey; he could not remember the exact date that John had died in the crash.

He thought about the many he had lost both before 1972 and between 1972 and 2028.

That included Paddy himself, yet Paddy had warned Al about saying anything about the future so he would not tell him anything about his future life and death.

In 2028, Al knew things that he should not have known and should not tell to people in 1972. He felt sure they would not want to know, despite so many that said they wished they could know the future.

Life and death, the inevitability, destiny, time-lines, were not always the way people wished it and the way people wished it was certainly not always the best way.

And in 2028, there were so many that he did not know where they were, if they still survived and what had happened. Despite having searched media such as

Facebook, many he never found.

Growing older is easier when it's slow, day by day, but jumping back and forward over fifty years is not always going to be fun, although he would not swap the twenty-four hours with Suomi for the world.

So he fell asleep crying for his losses.

Chapter 4: The Scramble

Al was on the bus about to arrive close to the venue where he was due to meet Suomi at a Donovan concert with an audience of one thousand and to which Suomi and Al had received an invitation.

He was looking forward to it;

He knew that it was going to be a fairly long walk from the bus stop to the hall but he had been told to simply follow the signs.

First he had to cross a large area of shrubland, mostly full of weeds and cacti, which was strange for Norwich but climate change had brought new plants to the county.

It was a much longer walk than he had thought.

Either side of him at some distance away, were huge jagged cliffs that seemed to reach the clouds.

Apart from the plants, he saw small wooden shacks, many painted in bright colours, some flying rainbow or peace symbol flags, some with brightly-dressed hippy-looking young people either attending small gardens of vegetables and flowers or simply sitting in the sun. Many waved at him, shouting "Good Luck", or "Keep on trucking" or "Follow your heart" and in one garden a massive sign reading "Never Give Up".

That was to his left side. To his right he spotted several small stalls displaying craftwork and foodstuff.

He headed for one piled with thick books and folders to confirm that he was heading in the right direction.

As he approached the stall, a young guy with long dark hair and a thick black beard beckoned him forwards.

The man explained that he was seeking sponsorship for his new invention, which he called fuelless flight. Somehow the technology that enabled flight was connected to the human brain and the claim was simply that it enabled and technicized telepathic controls, natural but until now hardly enabled human abilities.

Al was indeed sceptical and anyway had no money to invest, despite the chap's enthusiasm and brightly coloured A4 pamphlets. He asked the way. The guy pointed to the cliffs and said to go ahead on to the right side, find the steps, follow the people upwards and just keep going.

As Al found the people climbing the wide stone steps, he noticed that the people were all wearing boots and some carried ropes, whereas he himself wore socks and sandals and had no ropes. Yet he was an experienced climber from his University rock-climbing and fell walking club, when he had visited such as Snowdonia, the Lake District and Ben Nevis and he was sure the others would help him with their ropes if necessary, as is the spirit.

The steps looked well worn. Many thousands of people must have been this way.

How difficult could it be?

It looked like maybe one hundred steps before they would reach the top of this section. Then, presumably, there may be a scramble that meant some of the older people would need ropes. So off he set.

A hundred or so steps was not so hard and did not take long. Al's legs didn't even tire.

Yet as he reached the top, he saw indeed that the steps went down a way and led to a path that went round the next cliff and he could see another higher cliff beyond.

The path round this cliff face was a little narrow and muddy. Yet he would carry on. There seemed to be less people here though. Al wondered where the others had gone. There didn't seem to have been any other route to take.

At the end of this path was a steep path heading up to the next peak. Mostly narrow but walkable but requiring a scramble at some points.

He could see a girl with long blond hair scrambling up a scree slope in the distance. It looked like Suomi.

It seemed like hours of trudging and scrambling along tracks and ever-narrowing ledges, sometimes jumping across gaps with huge drops to the ragged rocks below. Al could see very few people now, none with ropes.

He spotted one chap way ahead on a higher rock face, climbing slowly to what now looked like the very top. Where was this place?

Why was it so difficult, so risky, danger of falling toe one's death with almost every step? Why would Donovan play up here?

Al did indeed now think he was doomed.

It was so steep and so slippery with mud and he was still in socks and sandals.

He thought he'd never make it and was filled with despair.

All he could do was cry for help. What a god-forsaken place this was. Up high but down so low. So close to Suomi but so far. Through hell seeking heaven.

The song kept going though his head 'First there is a mountain, then there is no mountain, then there is.'

Al wondered how Suomi would have gotten past this point and began to worry in case she had fallen.

Then he woke up in a panic.

Chapter 5: India

Al was looking out of the window of the room high up in the semi-luxury five star hotel he and Suomi, his friend, had rented for two weeks on the outskirts of Delhi.

Suomi had left about three hours ago to visit a local market, quite close to the hotel, to buy a couple of colourful head scarfs and Al was getting concerned as she had not yet returned. So he was looking out of the window. Not that he could see her from here. He was twelve stories up.

What he could see was amazing though. He had a clear view looking down over the five level highway that ran passed the hotel.

The lowest level was reserved for heavy goods, taxis and other motorised delivery vehicles and there were exit and entry roads that led to and from the ground level doors of the hotel and round to the backside of the building, as they called it.

The next level up was for buses and cars, again with exit and entry roads. Above that, the road was reserved for rickshaws and tut-tuts as they called them, both motorised and bicycle.. The top level was for horse-drawn vehicles, donkeys loaded with goods and even elephants. That was the only level open to the air above and the only level where people could walk.

There were no exit roads there, but Al knew that there were elevators along the road, large enough to move animals and carts all the way to the ground, even the elephants.

Al thought it was magnificent, and better still, it seemed to work. It all flowed smoothly. There were no traffic jams even though every road level was full of traffic, day and night. There were, he was told, no accidents and India was very proud of the achievement, even if it did sway in the wind.

Beyond that, that is from this height well above the top level road, Al could see all the way to Delhi.

Hard to believe the view. There were towers and other strange magical stone structures of all colours with flags flying, high up in the sky, magically suspended in the air. That was a major tourist attraction that brought many tens of thousands of people to the hotels alongside the road system, all with superb views. How they kept them floating in the air was a secret. They certainly looked solid and the authorities and hotel management alike insisted that they were, but Al thought surely an optical illusion or huge massive balloons.

After a while, Al decided to take the elevator down and venture outside and see if he could find Suomi. He would leave a message on the door asking that she wait in the chai bar and he would be back. That is what he did.

He found himself walking alongside stalls in a market selling brightly coloured fruit and vegetables. There were huge red, green and yellow mangoes, even bigger melons, oranges and bananas, bright carrots, aubergines, green vegetables. There were stalls selling juices of many kinds, lassi drinks, smoking and steaming dished of food and pots of chai with the characteristic smoky spicy smell, and stalls with huge piles of the spices themselves.

Further along there were stalls with bright cloths, textile rolls, many with scarfs and saris, cheap jewellery, pots and pans of all sizes and even birds in cages.

There was no meat to be seen. This was a vegetarian area. Al saw no leather goods either so maybe it was even vegan. Not unusual for India.

Al reached the end of the market but there had been no sighting of Suomi. He spotted a large tent a little way on, with a sign that said Chai Nirvana, just the sort of place Suomi may go for a drink.

So he headed over and, pulling the heavy drapes aside, ducked down through the drapes and went inside. There was a sweet aroma about the place, not the smell of spice and smoky chai he expected.

He spotted several men, naked above the waist and quite fat and sweaty looking, laying on rough wooden beds and mattresses on the floor. They were smoking opium. This was an opium den.

Quickly he decided to go back to the hotel. On the way he spotted Suomi.

“Suomi, quick, let’s get out of here. I don’t think it’s safe and it’s getting dark. He led her by the hand towards the overland and cable car transport that took people about Delhi, to get back to their hotel.

Hardly before they knew it they were whizzing along the tracks and then rapidly ascending high into the air.

The carriage, now quite rickety and made from wood, came to an abrupt stop and the door opened.

But this wasn’t their hotel.

It was the rooftop of the Arts building of UEA, Al’s University.

“Look!”, said Suomi, “There’s our hotel, I can see our room! It’s the other side of that mountain. How we going to get over there? It’s dark now!”

“I don’t know,” said Al, we obviously can’t walk it, we’re going to have to wait here ‘til the morning”.

Chapter 6: Ye Olde Norwich Festival

Al got off the bus. He had been talking to a young blond and beautiful French girl. She must have been in her early twenties. He was in his early seventies. He was 72.

She had explained to him that her boyfriend had left her so she had decided to come on this trip alone.

They had arrived in Tombland and now had to walk just about half a mile up Magdalen Street to Anglia Square to catch the coach for the next part of the 'Mystery Tour'.

The young girl suggested that they walk together which was fine with Al; despite her break-up she was happy and bubbly.

"What's your name?" he asked.

"Suomi" she said.

"Ha! If only Suomi!" he laughed.

Suomi giggled and took Al's arm in a friendly way but not as if helping him walk or anything like that. He liked that.

"I'm Al," he said.

"I know that" she said.

As they walked up the road passed the Maids Head hotel, she said "Let's go the back way, we 'ave some 'ours and they will wait."

She dropped her aitches in a delightful French way.

So they turned to their right and climbed and clambered through a bracken-covered path behind the Old Church until they were higher than the Church itself and could look down upon the street. That wasn't easy for old Al. "Oh to be young again," he said, "it was so easy back then", as he watched Suomi almost bouncing along. But he was glad she wasn't constantly offering to help him.

The path up here was wandering not straight, quite narrow in places and always rough under foot but well trodden. In places there was quite a drop to his left.

There were men walking about carrying planks of wood or buckets and others, men and women, on their knees to his right side as if on some sort of archaeological dig before the building work started.

To his left he could still see down between the gaps in the row of shops, to the street.

Suddenly Suomi pointed to their right and said "Look, Ye Olde Norwich Festival. Let's go there".

Al saw the large wooden gates with the sign above so "OK, pourquoi pas?"

"D'accord," she said.

As they entered through the gates there was a counter to buy the tickets, but the lady there just said "Go on through." They went through another but smaller set of wooden doors and came into a series of narrow streets with wooden fences either side, crowded with people that looked Indian and Arabian, with items of clothing strewn about on the ground. There was hardly room to pass by in some places but they did manage it and went through a series of several wooden doors or metal gates. He wasn't sure if people were selling stuff or just making a mess.

They came out into a larger street with stalls on each side but he couldn't make out what they were selling, but they were selling something. Definitely one was selling smoky tea.

To his right he spotted another huge set of wooden gates that were open. He could see inside an area at least two or three times the size of a soccer pitch with large wooden fences and large doors all the way round. He could see men that looked like referees from a wrestling match.

But the wrestlers were not humans, they were animals. He spotted a lion viciously attacking a small elephant. Then he saw a small giraffe running and it did a sort of drop-kick into a llama. There were rhinos and even crocodiles, dogs and bulls charging about, seemingly attacking each other at random. A large lion stopped and looked at Al. A referee ran to it with a whip and the animal ran off. It was chaos. Strangely there was no blood.

As stood watching for a good ten minutes or so when he noticed that Suomi had gone. He couldn't see her anywhere.
"Oh well, que sera sera"

So Al carried on walking to some more wooden gates and came out into a large field.

This one was not nearly so crowded and had more organised stalls selling antiques, statuettes, banners and flags, brass wares, rugs and small boxes, large silver-looking jugs and pots and pans, with some beautiful but massive brass trays. He didn't want to buy anything.

He looked around for Suomi but she wasn't there.

In the distance he spotted the Citadel. He remembered being there before. One had to climb down into a labyrinth that went on and on and he had been down there and almost got lost in the dark and dank passageways.

He didn't want to go in there again.

So he decided to head on to Anglia Square where he expected to find the coach and, hopefully, Suomi.

The next thing he knew he was waking up alone in his bed.

Now, that, he thought, was weird.

Chapter 7: 2028

Al had first met Daniel and Rebecca, whom they called Becky, in 2010.

They had been introduced by their mutual friend, Paddy. Daniel was wheelchair bound since his serious car crash in the 1980's, but was a jolly chap. They lived in Leeds. Al had only been to Leeds once, for a day, in 2003. He had almost gone there to the University in 1968, to study for a Chemistry degree, but had chosen UEA in Norwich instead.

It wasn't until after Paddy's death in 2014 that Al had started writing a series of various books. Amongst these was the true life story of his overland trip to India in 1972, supposedly written by a hat called Myhat and called "All About My Hat, the Hippy Trail, 1972" and Daniel and Becky became fascinated by the story.

Two other books written by Al were also of interest to them, in particular as they involved time travel: "Myhat in Egypt, Through the Eyes of a God" and "The Effie Enigma, The Motherless Mothers".

They were of interest because Daniel had been working on time travel since his time in Switzerland in the late 1970's and then at a top secret university department in Leeds.

Way back in 1972, Daniel had planned with his colleagues to secure the services of Paddy, who was sworn to secrecy not just then but for the rest of his life, to rent an apartment and prepare to receive visitors.

Daniel himself was the first one to go, in 2025 and that was when he discovered that when he arrived back in 1972, where Paddy was waiting for him, that although his mind would eventually retain all the memories of his life, his new body would be of his natural age at that time, that is mid-twenties, although he actually looked much younger.

That was also when he realised that he could go back again, another time, with Rebecca and they could live their lives together again and he could possibly avoid the car crash that had crippled him.

That visit was just for a few days, enough time to enable him to send information to his other self, working at Leeds, that would accelerate the development of the temporal technology, without ever having the two Daniels meet in person and without passing on any other information to them, to Paddy or anyone else, about any details of the future. He had to explain to Paddy that he could not give him “football pools” results or anything else, or advise on investments, that would make him rich, as also there was enough money already available in 1972 to pay Paddy an honest and substantial wage, so he would never have to work and could always be in Leeds at times that they agreed.

Daniel also realised then that when he returned to 2028,

his mind would return to the same crippled body that he had there and then.

But Al didn't know about Daniel's involvement with time travel experiments until 2026, when he had a visit from Daniel who broached the subject.

Daniel said "Al, I read your books about travelling to India in 1972 and your stories about the couple that went back to ancient Egypt and the story about Effie and people coming back from the future.

"Have you ever wondered, if time travel actually becomes possible one day, and of course if the human race and technology survives long enough, or aliens bring it, why we don't hear of people who came back?"

"Well," said Al, "there's that guy Elon Musk, he reckons he's from the future.

"And there's been others but they probably all got banged up in mental hospitals. And there were people who were supposed to be prophets like Nostradamus who either were from their own futures or had visions of the future.

"But I guess there's the problem of time paradoxes, if they do the wrong thing they could wipe themselves out so they could never be there to come back. You know that one about killing your own great grandfather before he had children?

"Though I always thought, well, if say your real great

grandfather was the milkman so the one you killed wasn't. That would work!"

Daniel laughed. "Yes, well there is that! They'd have to keep it secret and not tell anyone about the future, not go round making false millionaires through investments or gambling and not try to change the past. Imagine if somebody went back to kill Hitler which stopped the war. But we don't know what else would happen then, the world could end up worse, or we may have had a more capable tyrant in Germany and then they won the war!"

"Well there's lots of science fiction about multiple universes and diverging time streams." said Al. I remember the Doctor Who series when he used to say there are fixed points in time that could not be changed.

"He used to say time wasn't a straight line, it was a sort of curly-wurly, timey-whiney thing. And somebody else said it was like a tangled string. But they are just stories, like my book, of course Ed and Anna never actually went back four thousand years to Egypt!"

"Yes OK," said Daniel, "but *what if*? What if I gave you the chance to go back to 1972 for three days so long as you didn't meet yourself then or anyone you knew or try to change anything, then you come back here. What if you could be twenty-two again but keep your memories of the last fifty-six years since then?

"Where would you go? You couldn't go to Norwich or risk meeting yourself or anyone else on your India trip, or anyone you met before then? You couldn't for example, put money in the bank and get the interest now.

"You couldn't leave any information or advice for yourself or anyone else. Not stop anyone dying, see your parents. You couldn't tell anyone you were from the future!"

"Well, I guess so. I guess it would be good to be young again. Maybe I could see a band I enjoyed, somewhere else!" he laughed.

"Well," said Daniel, "Have I got a surprise for you.

"We thought about this and you're the one we want to take. It *is* possible and I have done it, been there and come back. I worked on this for over sixty years, set it up, and Rebecca and I are going soon, to Leeds 1972. We lived there then so we can't stay and for us it will be a one-way trip. I was young again, I could walk again. Want to come with us? But you'll only stay for three days."

"You're either dreaming or kidding mate" What proof you got?"

Chapter 8: The Trip

The date was set for February 14th 2028 but it was nothing other than coincidence that it was Saint Valentines Day.

Three people, Al, Daniel and his beautiful wife Rebecca, would make the journey to 1972.

For Al is was to be an experience, observation and report, trip of no more than seventy-two hours. Seventy-two hours in 1972!!

That was the limit set at the moment for a two-way trip, before the algorithms would start to degrade, Daniel had said and after that there would be no return. Then there would be two Al's in the world which pose all sorts of risk of paradoxes.

However, for Daniel and Rebecca it was to be one way, the first of its kind.

Daniel had lived his life paralysed from the waist down, despite cybernetics and artificial limbs, he had never been able to walk since his car crashed back in 1985 and Rebecca had been his devoted wife and nurse, although she had "played around" with Daniel's full knowledge and approval. He had always said that he did not want his own dreadful fate to hinder her full enjoyment of her life, so long as it did not go beyond "play", which included casual but safe sexual activities.

Thanks to Daniel's brain and Rebecca's enthusiasm, they had both made over a trillion dollars, well enough to pay for their trip and Al's.

The rules were simple: they had not to get involved with their own selves, their friends or families. They had to live their own lives. They had not to take advantage of any knowledge of events between 1972 and 2028. They had to avoid, at all costs, changing events or the lives of others.

In return they had the opportunity of living new lives under new names and with rejuvenated bodies. Daniel 2028 would not be changed, under strict observance of the rules set to avoid time paradoxes; Daniel 2028 would not be changed in any ways, he would still be rich, crippled and married to Rebecca. He and her would simply cease to exist from the time they departed.

But Daniel 1972 would be able to try to avoid one thing in particular, the car crash that had crippled him. Daniel and Rebecca 1972, they hoped would live a long and healthy new life.

Al, on the other hand, although existing twice, so to speak, in 1972, was to return to 2028. His life would not change provided he kept away from his "other self" and events associated with him. Despite his knowledge of the events between the dates, he would not invest, attempt to change anything or in any way do more than observe and report, and he had to return on time. Simple enough.

He was fascinated by 1972. Al had been born in 1950 and, by the end of 1972, had graduated at university in Chemistry, travelled overland on the so-called "Hippie Trail", found a teacher who had shown him how to find inner peace. Like many young people, Al had taken drugs like cannabis and LSD.

By 2028, Al spent time in prison, written several books and been through several relationships that had not lasted.

He had no children but plenty of friends. He had lived through the pandemics and remained in reasonable health for a 78-year-old. In short, he was happy with his life and felt that there was nothing he wanted to change.

None of the events that had happened to him between 1972 and now, or even before 1972, would be relevant and best forgotten, like a dream.

He had loved 1972 in particular and just wanted to see it again. That was why he had accepted Daniel's and Rebecca's offer to pay for his trip.

To avoid conflict with their own 1972 selves, they were set to land in Leeds in a house near the train station.

All Al had to do, according to Daniel, was to drink a potion that would enable him to sleep for seven days and trust in the Project, which he said was called 'The Mission' engineers to do the rest. He would wake up in 1972 in Leeds and would be met by somebody that would help him adjust and give him some money, maps, advice etc. Al would stay there for seventy-two hours and then be automatically brought back to 2028 when he would sleep for another 4 days to enable his body and mind to readjust. It was most important that he did nothing to change the future or to contact anybody that knew the original Al who would continue living his own time path life. That was why he, Al, now in 2028, knew nothing of himself going back until now and after all, he, now, was the original Al. He must not change things, he must return. Daniel and Rebecca, as he had said, would not be returning.

Chapter 9: The Returning

Al awoke from a deep sleep.

He had been dreaming that he was in 1972, that he had been in love with a gorgeous French girl called Suomi, a chemistry student but had to leave her. He had fallen in love.

He was in some sort of hospital bed with bars. Was he insane?

He was crying, deeply upset, like he'd suddenly lost a lover for ever. He couldn't stop sobbing even though he knew it was just a dream. It seemed so real. It was like it had gone on for days. His old friend Paddy had been there too. In Leeds. And Daniel and Becky. And he had been to a Donovan concert and made love with the most beautiful, wonderful girl he'd ever met. He had been in Leeds in 1972. Then he'd been ripped away and came back here.

Now he was here in Leeds in 2028, 78 years-old again. He'd been happy with his life. Now he was sad.

After a while a doctor appeared. Well Al assumed he was a doctor because he wore a white coat. He approached Al.

"Good morning Al and welcome back. My name is Doctor John Sullivan. I expect you are feeling tired and confused. It's only natural and it will pass. You've been asleep here for a week."

"Where am I?" asked Al.

"Am I in hospital? Am I crazy? Have I had some sort of accident. I just woke up crying. I had a very vivid dream."

As he rubbed his eyes and became more awake and alert, he was remembering more of the dream. Dreams normally faded with time but this one was starting to be more like a memory. He was questioning reality. Was that the dream or was this the dream? Or a dream within a dream. How would he know what was real. After all, he still had the feelings for the girl Suomi in 1972, but that was fifty-six years ago.

Al remembered Daniel and Becky. He remembered Daniel's promise of a journey back through time. He remembered he had taken some sort of narcotic to make him sleep for a week. He thought that was just a play on words. Had he been hypnotised? Was he in some sort of trip? He'd never had any sort of trip like this before. Not even a dream like this. It was like living science fiction. He half expected this Doctor John to be Doctor Who. He looked around the ward again in case there was a TARDIS. There wasn't.

Doctor John smiled and said: "Al, don't worry. It was real. You did go back to 1972. Your body and brain stayed here, sleeping. We made a new young body and brain for you. WE even had made a pair of spectacles, just like the ones that you used to wear back then, same style, same prescription, we which obtained from your opticians in Norwich.

The couple that you you went to 1972, we call with Daniel 1 and Rebecca 1. You came back alone. They wanted to stay there and make new lives for themselves. Daniel 1 was not expected to live another week but Daniel 2 had a fresh start".

"So where are they now?"

"The two we sent back? We don't exactly know. Initially they went to India and then on to Australia. We stopped tracking them in the 1980's.

Their bodies here of course deteriorated after three days and after six days, they died, both of them. They were cremated in secret yesterday. Those two individuals no longer exist in 2028.

"Rebecca, who we'll call Rebecca 2, has lived through her life again and survived. Sadly, though, Daniel 2 passed away in 1999, from an illness. He did not get crippled in a crash but he did not live as long as Daniel 1. Strange isn't it?

"But now you must rest again. We will bring you some food and I will come back after lunch, about two o'clock. That will give you time to absorb this reality!"

Doctor John left and Al got dressed and washed in a side-chamber bathroom and then lay on the bed mussing events. They brought him a vegetable curry and rice for lunch, with Kulfi ice cream!. It wasn't long before he fell asleep again.

Chapter 10: The Alarm

Al woke up in the middle of the night because his alarm clock was beeping: 'Beep, beep, beep, beep'

He was on a coach moving down a roadway quite fast and it was pitch black outside. His first thought was to simply stop the alarm before it woke up too many of his fellow passengers although whoever was sat next to him did not stir.

He wondered why he had set the clock anyway, it wasn't as if he had to get up. It must have been set accidentally.

He had to switch it off. He did not want to wake Suomi, who was asleep with her head on his shoulder, or wake the other passengers.

So he pulled it out of his bag and switched off the alarm.

But it kept on beeping, the switch just did nothing.

So he decided to remove the battery from the section at the back of the clock. He did that but it kept on 'Beep, beep, beep, beep ...'

What a nuisance. He'd have to take the clock apart. He removed the plastic bit covering the clock face and in desperation pulled off the minute hand.

Still 'Beep, beep, beep, beep... '

Then he woke up.

His alarm clock was beeping: 'Beep, beep, beep, beep'

He was still on a coach moving down a roadway quite fast and it was pitch black outside. His first thought was to stop the alarm before it woke Suomi or any of his fellow passengers although whoever was sat next to him did not stir. This was a déjà vu.

Then the person in the front seat turned and said "Please turn that off. It is waking people up. We don't need it." It was Rebecca, an elderly friend.

He wondered why he had set the clock anyway, it wasn't as if he had to get up. It must have been set accidentally.

So he pulled it out of his bag and switched off the alarm.

Surely this was a déjà vu?.

But it kept on beeping, the switch just did nothing.

So he decided to remove the battery from the section at the back of the clock. He did that but it kept on 'Beep, beep, beep, beep ...'

What a nuisance. He'd have to take the clock apart.

He removed the plastic bit covering the clock face and in desperation pulled off the minute hand. Still 'Beep, beep, beep, beep… '

Now he sat there with a clock hand in each of his hands, both beeping loudly.

He laughed out loud and said to himself "This is just a dream, I'm just in bed in Norwich and my clock there is waking me up!"

He wanted to wake up Suomi and tell her.

Then he himself woke up, again.

His first thought was "Am I awake or still dreaming?"

It was like dreams within dreams, very confusing and he felt like he was switching between realities. Not a pleasant feeling at all.

It was dark in the room, the middle of the night.

He switched on the bedside lamp, got out of bed and went downstairs to make a cup of tea. Only then did the fogginess start to clear.

Chapter 11: Suomi

Al awoke from the dream. This time he knew he had been dreaming. He was back in the hospital room in 2028. He was elderly again. But he felt good and refreshed.

It was not long before Doctor John came back.

“Before anything else, I want to show you some photographs from 1972. We have agents there and they had to keep an eye on you to make sure you did not break the rules or risk the future, or even die. And they followed you about and took pictures. They’re black and white but from a 1972 camera, a good one for the time.

“Look this one is you and Paddy and Daniel and Rebecca together.

“And here’s one of you leaving Paddy’s place on the High Street, walking along the street, catching the bus. Inside the station and down by the river. And this one is of you sitting in the Square. You look a bit despondent in this.

“And this one is of you going into a post office. You posted an envelope with ten pounds to yourself in New

Delhi. We let that get through. It wasn't really changing any time lines because in your memory on that day, it had already happened and stopping it may have caused changes.

"You walked the streets a while and went to the train station."

"Yes it was all quite crowded" said Al.

"Now here's one of you and Paddy in the Fforde Grene pub. You were drinking the old Newcastle Brown ale.

Now this is the next day, the Saturday, of you in Woolworth's Kwik café, look you are sitting talking to the French girl, Suomi. And then you and her went to the music hall in a booth listening to some songs from an LP. Donovan was, it? Remember,? She bought it and you bought a Jimi Hendrix LP.

"

Then you went on a bus to Roundhay Park. It's still open today, a big attraction in Leeds. You walked round and sat by the Waterloo Lake."

"Here's you together hand-in-hand walking by the lake, you were watching a few men fishing. Then here's one of you sitting close in the park listening to some hippies playing acoustic guitars and hand-drums.

"That night we have you both eating curries in an Indian restaurant – that's why we gave you curry for lunch.

"These are a bit darker. They are you two together in the student union watching the Donovan performance. Look, Suomi is kissing you."

Al started to cry.

"Don't cry, "said Doctor John, "this is supposed to be a happy occasion. These photos are over fifty years old."

"Yes," said Al, "But for me it was just a week ago. I

didn't want o leave her. I loved her. I loved everything about her. And I was so young again. Do you have any more?"

"Yes there's lots but these are the best ones. I know you both went back to her flat and stayed the night. We don't have any from inside there."

The Doctor said: "Now, If you feel up to it Al, we have another surprise for you. You have two visitors"

"Yes I am fine, who is it?"

The Doctor smiled: "It's two elderly ladies. One is Rebecca 2. She came back to the UK in the early part of this century and met Paddy again and now she is here and wants to see you again."

"Wow, do you think that's OK because it might mess up some time line or something?"

"No it's fine, because there is only one of her now.

"For the sake of clarity, the elderly Rebecca and Daniel that you met years ago, friends of Paddy, we call Rebecca 1 and Daniel 1, the one that originally couple that went back with you but left their bodies here, no longer exist. This is the Rebecca 2, as we call her, the Becky that you were in 1972 with, when you went back. She has aged again. She is in her late seventies now. It's not always easy to explain. From 1972 until Becky 1's body dies, there were two Rebecca's and we had to ensure they never met. This Rebecca, Rebecca 2, was printed in 1972."

"Yes it'll be weird but yes let her in."

The Doctor left the ward and soon came back with the two ladies. One was clearly Rebecca, she looked much the same as she had looked a week ago. It could be the same woman, Al thought, this could still be some sort of hoax or con, but why? So, this was supposed to be Rebecca 2, who had in fact lived almost two lives, and Rebecca 1 no longer existed?

The other woman he didn't know, but she did have a familiar look about her as well. Al struggled to think who she was.

Rebecca strode quickly across the room and hugged Al. "It's so good to see you again Al, after all these years."

Rebecca stood back and smiled. "This," she said, "is Suomi!"

Chapter 12: The Returning Returnings

Al was amazed, shocked, surprised, overjoyed, sad, all at the same time. He didn't know whether to laugh or cry.

Suomi was the last person he expected to see ever again.

After all, he had been prohibited from telling her that he was 'from the future', back in 1972. He was not supposed to tell her or anyone else, It was only Paddy, Becky 2 and Daniel 2 and maybe a few technicians back then, that knew, and Becky and Daniel were supposed to have left Leeds and never returned.

Now she is here with Rebecca 2, the "new Becky", but now she has aged again.

Suomi still had the same air, vibe, about her, she still had the same attractiveness and Al was still attracted to her.

He vowed never to abandon her again, if he had any choice.

"But how did you get here Suomi?" he asked.

"How did you find me? How did you even meet Becky? What's happened? What's happening? Am I dreaming? Are we in 1972 and I'm dreaming I'm old?"

"Life is but a dream." laughed Suomi, "but this is real. We are really here! I also 'ave so many question!"

She still drops her ''aitches" he laughed to himself. She still has her accent.

"I 'ave 'undreds of stories, Al and I want also to 'ear about your life. Me, after you 'ad to go and then I saw Paddy, and 'e said you 'ad to go to Africa and 'he did not know where, I did cry, but Paddy, 'e said you 'ad told 'im to look after me. Then when I was a graduate in the chemistry in Leeds, I 'oped you were coming back and I was a teacher in chemistry in a school. Paddy, 'e was always there for me when I needed 'elp. But I thought you were died, I mean dead, and I just 'ad to get on with my life, like 'e said.

"Al I was married four times but they did not make me 'appy. First time in Leeds but after five years we 'ad a divorce. Then Il went to India and Nepal and smoked the chillums with the Sadhu's and tried the meditations and then I went to Thailand and met my second 'usband and we lived there a while, then I 'ad to get divorced because 'e beat me, that Thai man. 'E said he was a Buddhist but 'e was not at peace. I went to Japan and then to Australia and I met another man, a good man, Graham, and I married 'im for ten years. Then Graham, 'e was ill and 'e died of the cancer.

"But I was not really 'appy there. Then I 'eard about my Guru, Maharaji, now we call 'im Prem, it means love but it's 'is name. That made me feel peace. In Australia I 'ad a letter from Paddy and 'e said 'is friends Becky and Danny were in Perth, so I met them and then Danny, 'e died too, in 1999 I think. Becky came to live with me. I was a teacher of the French and the science in Sydney.

"Then me and Becky, we went to France in the south and I was teacher there too, of the sciences.

I used to see a lot of Paddy, 'e always 'elped me and I likes 'im a lot. When 'he got busted going out of Maroc on his coach with all that 'ashish, it was a lot, they put 'im in prison and when I 'eard I went to Tangiers and lived there and went to see ''m and took 'im some food. To start with 'e at to sleep on the floor in a room with other men but I gave 'im some money so he could buy a bed. Funny that ''e said he could get free ''ashish in there but 'ad to buy 'is own bed."

"Yes I remember that," said Al interrupting her, "I heard he was banged up after he'd been there about a year. I was in Norwich and wrote to him. He wrote back and said he was being looked after and his daughter was living there. He had prostrate cancer and eventually the King of Morocco gave a pardon to some prisoners and he was released early. He came back to Norwich. He was a great man, told fantastic stories and always wanted to help people even though he couldn't tolerate fools and bullies. I went to Switzerland with him once, for a week and when we were at the airport waiting to fly home, he asked how much I spent, and when I told him he counted out the money then and there and insisted I take it.

I went to Egypt with him too, for two weeks in Luxor in 2010. He used to take a big teapot to breakfast in the hotel and fill it up and sit for hours drinking it and reading the English and French papers. I got up and went to breakfast and he'd already been there for two hours!

"We had a bungalow in the grounds. I remember one evening at dinner the hotel manager, a German, came round and asked if everything was good. Paddy said no and the guy took out a notebook and pencil and asked what was wrong. "We've been here three days and we've only had beetroot once!", he said. The manager wrote it down and said that from now one we'd have beetroot every day and he would get some done by his mother's recipe. And we did!

"That hotel was on King's Island, it used to be called Crocodile Island but there were no crocs there any more. They grew a lot of their own fruit and vegetables and had mostly there own eggs. Every night it was a different themed meal. But me and Paddy, we ate loads and after two weeks we both had swollen bellies. I have a photo of us, I'll show you, it's here on my cell phone.

"I have lots more photos, I'll show you later.

By the time we left Luxor it was thirty-eight degrees. When we got back to Gatwick airport about midnight it was minus five!

“I was sad when Paddy died, but we all must die.

“Anyway, sorry Suomi, you carry on.”

“That’s OK, Al, I love stories about Paddy”, she said.

“After I ‘ad been in France in the South, I got married again. Pierre that was but ‘e died after a year and I was very sad as two ‘usbands had die d and one we ’ad to ‘ave a divorce and one ‘e beat me lived there on my own until Paddy said to come back to Leeds in 2008, I think, and I lived here. I always remembered you, Al. I think I always love you too much from one day in 1972.

“Then Becky came back after Paddy died, in 2014 I think and I lived in an ‘ouse with ‘er and then about a week ago she said we were going to meet you again. And ‘ere we are!”

"So now I want to 'ear about you!"

Well," said Al, "Where to start? I was born in South Wales in 1950. My family were not rich but my parents did their best to bring us up and made sure I had a good education. I had one sister, three years younger than me. We lived in a big terraced house along with my mother's parents and one of her sisters.

"I went to a local school and became interested in chemistry. Well school was OK but I was quite shy. I was also interested in astronomy and even went train spotting and camping in South Wales. Funny enough I wasn't interested in travel. I did French and German in school, was not so keen, I thought why would I want to go to Germany. I failed my German 'O' level, but passed French. Well, after all, I did it for five years.

"When I got my 'A' Levels, I went to the University of East Anglia to do chemistry in 1968. I had Leeds on my list, like I said, but decided on Norwich.

"In 1972, before I met you, I had become a follower of Guru Maharaji, now mostly known as Prem Rawat, and practised the meditation he showed, and found a way to find peace inside and that helped me through inside and outside of prison. I still listen to him today.

"Like you I saw a lot of bands and met a lot of people.

"I gave up on politicians before I was old enough to even vote!. In fact I never voted until I was 42. I sort of got involved with my type of politics in 1999 when I cofounded the legalise cannabis alliance as a political party.

“I did that because I had been involved with cannabis since my last year at UEA when I started smoking it. I lived through the time when so many people were getting busted in their own homes, for possession, even though they were not actually doing any harm.

“For me it was all about human rights and freedom of choice and I already knew that the plant helped so many people. I had smoked it, sometimes in copious amounts, with all sorts of people from Sadhu's and Jains in India in 1972 – my other self which is actually me, was on the way to India when I met you Siomi in 1972. Weird eh? I smoked with hippies and travellers and businessmen and musicians, rich and poor, all sorts of people. I took acid in Kabul. They all seemed like decent people, well almost all, crooks smoked it too.

“In 1992 I went to prison for four and a half years of my life, out of the ten year sentence. That was for conspiracy to import and supply cannabis, ten years on each, concurrent.

“I spent ten months in HMP Whitemoor, then I was sent to HMP Blantyre House in Kent, a semi-open C cat where we all wore our own clothes as did the screws. It was based on trust and the day after arriving from max security I found myself on a two mile countryside ramble.

I carried on my computer studies and did other courses

and secured a Diploma in Computing at the Open University.

“I had been to Egypt in 1989 and 1990 and was fascinated by the history so wrote my first book “From Dot to Cleopatra’, a concise history.”

“Wow,” said Suomi, “I was In Egypt in 1990 to, in December I think. I went to Cairo to see the pyramids and museum and then went to Luxor to see the Temples and the tomb. It was fantastic.”

“We almost met then! Said Al. I was there in early February in 1989 and again in 1990!.

In Blantyre House, I volunteered for the Amenities Committee, formed a charity fund-raising group, organised two “Stir Crazy” days for Mencap, a mental health charity that helped people who were slow to develop in the brains and many also physically disadvantaged too, they came into the prison grounds with their carers, well over 1000 people and 90 prisoner volunteers.

“I played in a Christmas pantomime, I was a dwarf called Bumpy. That was funny. That was Snow White.

“I learned to organise people, and I learned to speak in public. I had been very shy, really, at UEA. That came in handy for the LCA.

“In 2001, I stood for Parliament on the cannabis issue with my own policies on everything else, in Norwich

South. I got about seven hundred votes, did radio and TV interviews etc, spoke before the Home Affairs Select Committee and debated at the Oxford Union. I also spoke at conventions, at a girls school and at universities. I stayed with the LCA until 2011, organising it.

"Also at Blantyre House, I wrote a report along with another inmate and the prison governor, Jim Semple, for his thesis at the Cambridge Institute of Criminology, later that became my second book, "Damage and Humanity in Custody". That was a more academic book but, I think, unique. Jim used to say "Don't call me Sir!"

"In 2014, I wrote my third book. "All About My Hat, The Hippy Train 1972", the story of my journey to India when I got sick..

"My good friend, John Sullivan, died in a car crash the evening after my friend Keith and I left them in Antalya, Turkey and my other friend, Mike, got badly hurt. I didn't know about that for months but met a guy Pete Roscoe on my way home after I got ill, in Kabul. He was on his way to India. I never saw Mike again.

"To earn money I used to travel and buy goods, from women's clothing to silk painting, boxes and brass to rugs and wooden stuff. I never made a fortune but always recovered the travel costs so I could travel again.

"I wrote a few other books about my Life. "Time for Cannabis, the Prison Years", "Out of Joint, 20 Years of

Campaigning For Cannabis", "Myhat in Egypt, Through the Eyes of a God" and the last one was "The Effie Enigma, The Motherless Mothers" a science fiction time travel story.

"Maybe I'll be able to read some to you one day.

"I am very much anti-government and the way they just walk over people's life. I see most of them as corrupt deviants, greedy tyrants and really want nothing to do with them.. With our two-party first-passed-the-post election system none of my votes have really made any difference at all.

"What they got up to with that Covid19 pandemic and so-called lockdowns was atrocious.

"Despite relationships and love affairs, I never got married or had any children that I know of, but who knows I may have, but I have two beautiful God-daughters, one living in Wales and one in Italy, and two other nieces in Wales. They all have two children each.

"I still live in Norwich, still trying to write.

"So I have enjoyed my life and I hope you have too. And I am glad I met all the people I have met. Most of all, I'm glad I met you and I am really happy you are here."
"Sounds like you 'ad a good life, Al. I am so 'appy you did and I am also 'appy to be 'ere."

Siomi leaned forwards and kissed Al, gently, on his lips.

Chapter 13: The Sky

Suomi and Al had gone to the University one night to watch the meteor shower and lightning.

They lay on the grass next to a tall building with big glass windows through which they could see students taking evening seminars.

Suomi herself was a teacher.

As it got dark it also got cold and Suomi invited him to share her unzipped double sleeping bag.

They lay together watching the skies. As the time passed, they huddled closer. It was very cold outside the bag. At one point Al slipped his cold hand around her and against her back, beneath her shirt that had ruffled up outside her jeans.

She gasped and moaned.

"You rascal," she said.

"That is so cold!", she laughed.

"Sorry, couldn't resist," laughed Al.

"I don't mind, I forgive you." Suomi pushed herself

closer but still side-by-side, both laying on their backs. There were lots of "ooh"'s and "aah" 's as the meteors shot across the sky, or the high distant lightning flashed.

Suomi laughed and said "Anyone who can 'ear us may think we're 'aving sex."

"If only," said Al, "but better not."

She turned on her side and he on his, facing each other, sharing breath and a kiss.

He was starting to doze off despite feeling somewhat stimulated by her warmth and closeness. He felt his own hardness pressing against her. He moved away.

Suomi moved closer again, and started making motions.

"Stop it!" said Al. "not here in public!"

They fell asleep. Well Al fell asleep. He assumed she did too.

When he awoke it was daylight and he still felt the Morning Glory. He moved away, got out of the double sleeping bag and stood up, trying to think of something else.

As Suomi stirred, he said quietly "Come on let's go and have breakfast and coffee."

"Look up at they sky," she said.

"There are lots of birds, flocks, flying 'igh up there!"

He could see them; thousands of them. He didn't know what sort of birds they were but they were big.

They were like large black clouds descending and it was only as they cam closer but still high above the building, that they actually looked like birds. Some were flying as if in a cloud, others in a V formation.

Some flew round and round. It was a spectacular show.

Next thing he knew, they were inside a building, walking along the corridor. Suomi was on his right side and another woman walking besides him on his left. He didn't know who she was.

As they approached a horizontal conveyor, the type they often have at large airports, both the women took his arms.

As soon as they stepped on the belt, it began to speed up. Faster and faster.

Now it was moving really fast. Everything became a blur. It was like a Star Trek spaceship as he had seen on TV, travelling faster than light, whirling round and round, speeding on he did knew nor where.

It was not a very comfortable feeling and he was glad that the three of them were holding each other upright. Suddenly it slowed down and stopped and as he stepped off, the woman on his left letting go of his arm but Suomi still clinging to his right, he saw that they were in a foyer with a corridor each side.

As he stood there he saw the people that looked mostly like students probably, walking about, and a coffee bar.

They went to the eating bar to get some "Café au Lait et un croissant".

After eating and drinking, she said, "Come on, we 'ave to go outside. I 'ave my car, I will give you a lift 'ome."

He wanted her.

He wondered what would happen next.

Chapter 14: Going Back

Al spent the next few days with both Suomi and Rebecca 2. They booked into a Leeds hotel all expenses paid by the Project. Suomi and Rebecca 2 shared a twin-bedded room and Al had a single. Al thought it was better that way. But he still had time to meet with Suomi on her own and chat about their lives. The three of them shared meals and drank fine wine.

The hotel was in the city centre near the station and was called The Dakota Leeds and was five star and had all the facilities that you would expect from a luxury hotel. Both rooms, which were adjacent, had views of the city. The rooms were grey and brown with framed pictures of old Leeds on the walls and subdued lighting, large colour TV, fridge, writing desk and Wi-Fi access. There was room service, laundry and almost anything legal available at the touch of a button. Reception staff were very friendly and helpful and the whole bill was prepaid.

The hotel had a quality bar and grill restaurant.

The Project had arranged for top quality vegetarian meals for Suomi and Al and Rebecca both had good fish.

The wine was excellent too.

They had a whole week there so could also go out to dine and the Project had arranged a list of recommended quality restaurants about the City along with a chauffeur-driven car at their disposal, each evening.

Al thought the food, the service, the décor, all superb.

Taxis were readily available and Al hoped that he and Suomi could visit the Roundhay Park again.

But his main concern was to talk to Suomi.

He had soon realised that he still loved her and her accent and mannerisms and really didn't want to lose her again. Sadly though, he knew only too well, losing loved ones was part of getting old.

He was wondering if they would be happy sharing the rest of their lives together, but he was also contemplating the possibility of them both going back to some time in their past, maybe not 1972, maybe not anywhere they had ever been before. He was thinking about Canada.

One day, Doctor John turned up and said he had four tickets to see a band and the four of them could go together.

The band was called 'The Dons of Avon' and were a Donovan tribute band. It was in a local pub.

The first song they played was "Sunshine Superman".

For Al it was only just over a week since he had been at the Donovan concert at Leeds University with Suomi.

For her of course, it was almost six decades.

Of course, the concert was very different. It wasn't Donovan but all the group, with a couple on guitars, a drummer, one on harmonica and a singer that sounded quite like the old Donovan they had seen, were all dressed hippy-like, colourful, just like the man himself.

This time the audience were all on seats and quite aged.] with a few younger people but Al thought the average age was over seventy. And people were drinking but there was no smoking, no smell of cannabis. He doubted anyone was tripping on acid.

Suomi said she had loved it.

Later that evening, they met up again with Doctor John in the hotel restaurant and Al put his idea to him.

He asked about the possibility of Suomi and himself going back in time again.

"But you both realise that after three days you will never be able to come back, even if you live older than you are now! In fact you haven't!

"We've only sent back two people under these conditions, Daniel and Rebecca and I'm sure Rebecca can tell you how difficult it was knowing that there were two of each of you, and for them knowing that the original Daniel, Daniel 1, shall we say, was to be involved in that car crash and that they would be able to do nothing to stop that. And that you could never have contact with friends or family outside of the Project. And your family and friends here would never know where you had gone. We will have to tell them that you died and arrange a cremation and funeral for your bodies.

"But it *is* possible. We would have to send you to a country that you have never visited and had no friends there.

"We will create for you two new identities with all the papers you'll need and get you registered as born and resident in that country.

"Of course we would provide finance but you would have to make your own way through your lives. We will maybe never know if you stay together or even if you survive. We may never know if you have children. Although we'll observe you for a while, you will really be on your own to make your lives as they go.

"We have no records, at least right now, as time goes with all the possible paradoxes, twists and turns, we haven't actually sent you back yet, though in another time line we have!, *We* don't know how long you will live, or should I say have lived. We don't even know that at some time in our future, we may see you again."

"For all we know, Alun 2 and Suomi 2, as we will refer to, the new ones, could be alive or dead. They could even walk in here tomorrow. Well, not just walk in, but try to. There could have been two of you for fifty years!

"And even if we knew what the new couple did, we wouldn't tell you, because you would remember when you get back in time, you would know your future, as that could lead to disaster.

"How about Canada?" Al and Suomi said at just about the same time.

"It is very 'ard for me to understand, but I do not 'ave a care. I want to go", said Suomi.

She laughed, "We will 'ave fun. We will be young again and together!"

That night they shared Al's double bed. They hugged and kissed but did not make love.

The following day Suomi went to Al's room.

"Becky 'as died in the night," she said. "The 'otel 'ave called the doctor and he 'ad an ambulance take her to an 'ospital. She 'as gone. We 'ad no chance to make our goodbye, but now maybe she is with Daniel again, and Paddy. I am very sad."

Suomi started to cry. Al hugged her until she stopped and then he phoned Doctor John.

A couple of days later, Doctor John came to the hotel again and told the couple that they would be making their journey the next day. Rebecca 2 would have been there to 'see them off' as they took their sleeping potions but now the Doctor said it was best if he himself was with them.

"When you wake up," said the Doctor, "you will be in a small quiet house on the outskirts of Vancouver, which is where we are sending you.. There will be a project employee there to meet you to help you acclimatize and learn what you should naturally know about the area, Canada, the history and the politics.

"You may be a little disorientated at first, which is why we'll have someone there to help, as Paddy did your first time. But your memories of your life and world events will return to you. You must never act upon them, never try to change anything, never contact anyone from your past or take advantage of the situation. Just like Daniel 2 never tried to stop the crash that Daniel 1 had been injured in. You must live new lives. I cannot stress that enough!

"You will be Alun 2 and Suomi 2.

"You will each have a considerable amount of cash and money in bank accounts, all the papers that you will need but no passports. The agent, who will serve as a maid is fully aware of the situation and will stay with you for up to six months at which time she will move on, sworn to secrecy."

The next day, in the evening, Doctor John turned up and he gave them each the drink.

Al was thinking to himself, this has been 56 years for Suomi but just about two weeks for me.

Suomi whispered to him “You ‘ave always been my sweetheart and you always will be. I want you to know that.”

“Et toi pour moi,” said Al.

They lay side-by-side on the huge double bed in Al’s room and together they drifted off to sleep.

THE END and THE BEGINNING.

Chapter 15: Dr John, SMILEY and Effie

It was the evening of a journey of a new lifetime for Suomi and Al when Doctor John had turned up at their hotel to make the preparations.

"Doctor John?" asked Al. "How does it all work."

"Well I'm no technician," said the Doctor, "and I won't pretend I know it all. I can just give you an outline, more of the history, if we can call it that as it's about past and future. Forgive me if I get my tenses mixed up," he laughed.

"Like most people that use computers, we use the technology but few of us actually know how it all works. It's to do with time tunnels, artificial intelligence, pure information transfer and Pure Information Clones which we call PICS. Oh and total mind download."

"Dr John," said Al, "I thought I would mention that you have the same name, John Sullivan, as my friend that died back in 1972 in Turkey. Is that just a coincidence?

"No Al, "smiled the Doctor, "I am actually the grandson of his brother! "But I'll start in the future!

"In the year 2250, there is, or will be, or was, a woman called Effie Zwanzig. Apparently there were lots of Effies and they all had numbers but I don't know which

Effie, came back to 2020, through time. By then they had progressed way beyond what we have now. She broke their own rules by bringing back information that enabled us to progress much faster than we would have. She also encouraged and enabled us to send back help and hints to 1968.

"Already there had been Effies, apparently, sent back to various times in human history to steer the human race towards expanding, eventually, into colonising the galaxy.

"And there were others, called QT's and DM's, which she called Quentin and Adam. She even told us that the first really intelligent members of Homo Sapiens Sapiens were Effiies and Adams, which she said our mythology calls Adam and Eve! Well, I know that is hard to believe

"One Quentin went back to help Albert Einstein and one Effie went back to work with Albert Hoffman, the man who invented LSD and who came up with the idea of Project Outreach, the concept of colonising the galaxy with humans. By 1943, after Einstein had left Germany which was under the rule of Adolf Hitler and the world was at war, Nazi scientists in an underground research facility at the Owl Mountains, were working on a time machine using rapidly spinning magnetic fields. That was their project called Die Glocke, named after the bell shaped chamber. Effie told us that it was with the help of another Effie that the Allied forces moved the equipment in secret to the Project Outreach facilities in the United States, where research continued.

"During the mid-twentieth century, masters such as Tesla, Turin and later Jobs and Musk, and the acid-head computer pioneers, began working on supercomputers and artificial intelligence. Others were working on wormholes and mind transfer, a way to record what is in a person's mind, their personalities, ambitions, memories and even their fears. The Artificial Intelligence they made, they called SMILEY, after acid-guru Timothy Leary's formula for what he saw as the future of the Human Race; in fact it was S, M, I squared, L, E which stands for Space Migration, Increased Intelligence, Life Extension; he also proposed the idea of seeding the stars.

"Already Outreach had become a reality. Apparently one of the Effies had met with and was said to have taken LSD with John F Kennedy, before he became president of the USA and before acid became more widely used, and inspired him to his eventual speech about sending man to the Moon and, quote 'doing those other things'. That may well be why Kennedy was assassinated in 1963.

"Our Effie also warned us that in the future the A.I. software, deep out in space, had become tyrannical and enslaved the human populations. To stop that, in other words to alter the future, we needed to install some sort of fail-safe and build in a mortality limit for SMILEY at 2250, after which time, she said, SMILEY would destroy itself and free the Human Race again.

"See what I mean about time paradox and how we need to try not to change our past? Even a small change could cause massive changes, not just to our present but to our future, and in a way changing the future could change the past. What if say, somebody did something that changed the future so that Project Outreach failed, or that SMILEY or Effie never existed, and those sent back to our history were never sent back. What if Adam and Effie never became Adam and Eve? What if the giant leaps for mankind never happened? What if Hoffman had never made LSD or Kennedy never taken it? We may not be here and now having this conversation. You may never have gone back to 1972.

“But I can only guess that as we are, those changes never happened. That’s why we keep telling you to be so careful. Even a small pebble can cause ripples in time and space! In fact, Effie told us that passing on the information to people in her past was OK because in her history, it had already happened.

“So now we have reached the stage where we have cracked the genomes, the genetic code, and we have achieved total mind download, pure information cloning and we have the technology to open a conduit between times, thanks to an off-shoot from the CERN accelerator work in Switzerland, which did in fact almost destroy the planet, according to Effie.

“We were able to send back information that would enable those in 1970, in our Project in Leeds, to accommodate the time conduit and create the technology such as 4D printers, to build new bodies rapidly, using the Pure Information Clone and Total Mind Downloads that we could transmit. So, you see, it's not actually you that is transmitted, it is your information, which is uploaded into the 4D printer to rapidly reproduce a younger body but with full memories, back in 1972.

"In short, thanks to the technology that Effie Zwanzig and others gave us, we progressed much much faster than we probably would have. We now have the technology to sort of beam people back and forth in time. It's not like the matter transporters in Science Fiction as in the old Star Trek films, it's more like sending emails of information of the essential DNA and mind and the complete mind code of the individual though a time vortex and printing a new body for them years ago. Like emails, the information is put together in the correct order when it arrives at the receiver.

"The new you, back in time, is what we call a Pure Information Clone.

"Project Outreach was started about a century ago by Albert Hoffman and Effie Vierzig, during the twentieth century and incorporated many projects including the Transhumanism Program to populate the galaxy. Effie Zwanzig said she was one of the results of the success of that. Also the search for true Artificial Intelligence, Total Mind Download and Bio-fabrication using 4D printers. It is the information of the person and the technology that we transport, not the person's body, although by the time of Effie Zwanzig, hundreds of years in the future, they perfected that too.

"So whilst the candidate is asleep, we copy the total

information of their brain, mind and DNA, send it through the time vortex, Bio-fabricate or print a new body at a specified age and using information that we can gather about them at that time ago, such as length or hair, body size-weight ratio, mind-set to some extent. Then we upload the Total Mind Download information into the new body and wait for them to wake up.

“As you know, AI, waking up may be a little confusing to start with, but all the memories return.

“Then, when it is time to come back to our present, we do the reverse, using your actual physical body that is still here, upload the mind information and wait for you to wake up again.

“As I said before, at present we can only keep your mindless body here alive for three days, then it dies. And your body back there decomposes too. That may sound scary Suomi, but AI will assure you that it is all perfectly safe. You’ll be be making a one-way trip as you wish.

“Don’t ask me how that actually works!”, he chuckled. “I guess at this stage we can say thank SMILEY, or thank Effie, or thank God!

“So far we have sent back a hundred people, just a couple of days each. Daniel and Becky were the first to not return..

“You two will be the second couple on a one way trip, a true second chance.”

All About My Hat

The "Hippy Trail" 1972

ALUN BUFFRY

MYHAT IN EGYPT

Through the Eyes of a God

ALUN BUFFRY

TIME FOR CANNABIS

The Prison Years

1991 to 1995

Alun Buffry

ALUN BUFFRY

THE EFFIE ENIGMA

THE MOTHERLESS MOTHERS

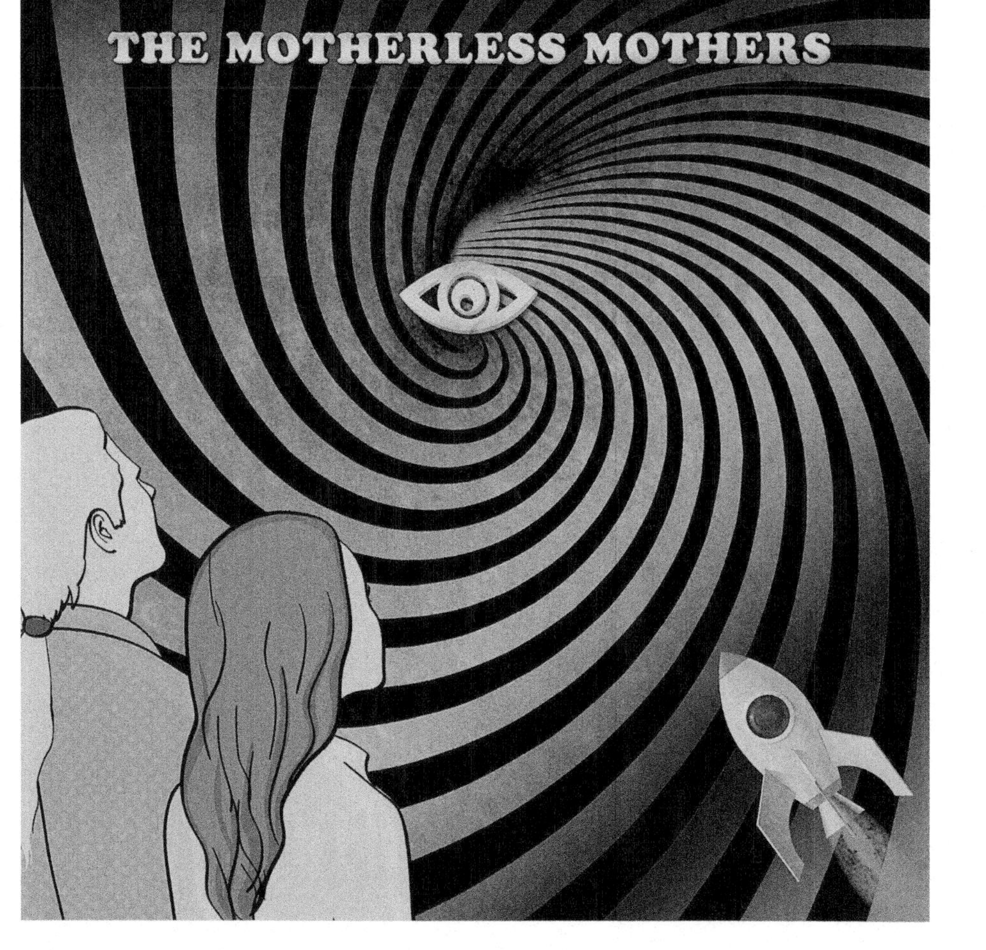

Printed in Great Britain
by Amazon